To writers and rhymers, everywhere
- Jay

To my loving and always supportive parents, Steve and Cheryl
- Erin

Lyric & Stone, LLC
LyricAndStonePublishing.com

ISBN 978-1-958514-06-1

Printed and bound in China

New Paige Press provides special discounts when purchased in larger volumes for premiums and promotional purposes, as well as for fundraising and educational use. Custom editions can also be created for special purposes. In addition, suuplemental teaching material can be provided upon request. For more information, please contact info@lyricandstone.com.

New Paige Press is an imprint of
LYRIC & STONE
PUBLISHING

Ricky, the rock that just Couldn't Rhyme

Written by
Ricky the Rock
(with a little help from Mr. Jay)

Illustrated by
Erin Wozniak

The sun shone above, and the air was quite cool,
as Ricky the rock was rolling through school.
He loved math and science, and gym was exciting,
so he rolled to his next class, which was reading and writing.

The teacher said,
"Class, I think that it's time,
for every rock here to learn how
to rhyme.

Rhyme is when words
all have the same sound,
like 'cat,' 'bat' and 'sat"...
there are lots to be found!"

Then she talked about oodles of poodles and noodles,
and how she loved freshly-baked warm apple strudels,
and claimed that a bear who had no fashion flair,
would eat an éclair if you made him a dare.

Ricky felt lost - his head started to spin.
So he turned 'round to talk to his friend, Tess the tin.
"Rhyming's confusing,"
Ricky said with a frown.
But Tess said,
"Cheer up,
and don't look so down.
You just need some practice -
you'll figure it out!
You'll learn how to rhyme -
I haven't a doubt."

Then suddenly Ricky was frozen with fright,
as his teacher said,

"class, I'd like you to write -
a fun rhyming story,
but don't get uptight,
I'd like you to write it
before bedtime tonight."

Rick said to Tess,
"What will I do now?
I have to write rhymes
and I just don't know how!"

Before Tess could tell him it would all be okay,
they heard a loud sound as the bell rang to say,
they had all reached the end of another fine day!
And Rick turned around and rolled sadly away.

Tess followed closely, "I'm sorry to pry...
But have you ever just thought that you might need to try?
For example," she said, refusing to yield,
as they passed an old farm and a wide open field,

"Can you think of a word that would rhyme with that cow?"

"Let's forget it," said Ricky,

"I just don't know how, and more to the point, I don't want to right now."

But Tess just pressed on,
"What rhymes with that truck?"

"You mean the one that looks stuck,
in the muck, with that duck?
I can't think of a rhyme...
but I wish him good luck!"

They rolled past a train yard, and Tess tried once more,
"I know you don't want to, and think it's a chore...
But what words would rhyme with that
small red caboose?"

"You mean the one over there,
near that moose on the loose?
I don't have a rhyme — I'm not Dr. Seuss!
Let's give this up now, it's simply no use."

"But Rick!"

exclaimed Tess, who went on to say,

"I guess you don't see...
you've been rhyming all day!
You're a natural, kid,
and I think you should know...
like the great Mr. Jay,
you're a lyrical pro!"

Ricky then realized that not trying was wrong -
He had no idea he could rhyme all along!

The next day at school, with a shy little smirk,
he went to his teacher and presented his work.
"I've finished my story, and it's really sublime,
Called 'Ricky, the Rock
            that Just Couldn't Rhyme'."

So Bria, the ladybug, who was there at the school,
was happy that Ricky had followed one rule:
we all have a talent that's hidden within,
and it's easy to find if we dare to begin.
Like Ricky discovered he was quite a good poet...
But like so many others, he just didn't....
Um...he just didn't....

Do you want Mr. Jay to read to your school?

Ask your teacher or principal
to email him at jay@meetmrjay.com